Would They Love a Lion?

To Saskia and Hanna

KINGFISHER

Larousse Kingfisher Chambers Inc.

95 Madison Avenue

New York, New York 10016

First hardcover edition 1995

First American paperback edition 1998

(HC) 2 4 6 8 10 9 7 5 3 1

(PB) 2 4 6 8 10 9 7 5 3

3(2TR)/0199/VAL/PW/CRM135

LIBRARY OF CONGRESS CATALOGING-IN-PUBLICATION DATA

Denton, Kady MacDonald.

Would they love a lion? / written and illustrated by Kady
MacDonald Denton.—1st American ed.

p.   cm.

Summary: Feeling neglected because of the family's new baby, Anna
transforms herself into different animals hoping to be noticed.

[1. Imagination—Fiction. 2. Babies—Fiction.] J. Title.

PZ7.D436Wo 1995

[E]—dc20   94–28576 CIP AC

ISBN 1-85697-546-0 (HC)

ISBN 0-7534-5018-6 (PB)

Designed by Chris Fraser

Printed in Italy

Would They Love a Lion?

• Kady MacDonald Denton •

KINGFISHER

NEW YORK

Anna dreamed she was a bird.
But when she woke up, she wasn't.

I could be a bird, said Anna. I could be.
And she flapped her wings.

I will be a bird.
And I'll have a nest.

A nest is too small, said Anna.
I want a cave. A big cave, a bear's cave.

I'll be a bear.

And Anna the bear growled
and went to breakfast.

A bear is too small,
said Anna.
No one notices a bear.
I'll be an elephant.

And Anna the elephant went outside
and thumped and swung her trunk.
But that isn't enough, said Anna.

I want to make the world shake.
I need to be bigger, really big, the biggest of all.
I'll be a huge . . .

dinosaur!

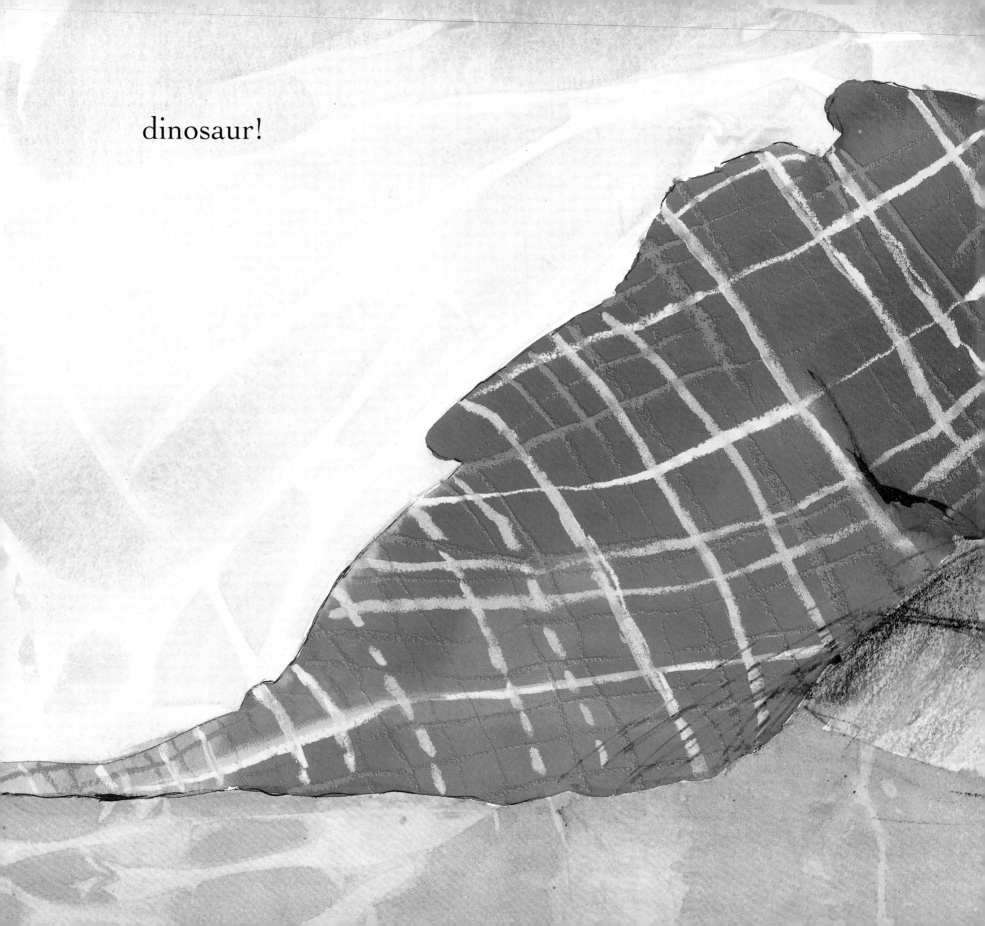

That's big, said Anna.
But now I'm all alone.
You can't cuddle a dinosaur.

I could be a rabbit. Everyone loves a rabbit.
And Anna the rabbit stopped for a kiss.
That's nice, said Anna. But . . .

A rabbit is too quiet.
I don't want to be quiet.
I want to play games.
I'll be a kitten—a cat—

A lion!
A lion loves to play.
Would they love a lion?

A lion can hide and a lion can roar.

Lions stalk.
Lions pounce.

Lions eat fast.
Lions run fast.

But lions get tired and love to sleep.
Would they love a lion?
Yes, they'd all love a lion.

And Anna the lion settled down for a nap.